BRENDA SANDERS

A BRENDA SANDERS PRODUCTION

A BIG
Thank you!

If you enjoyed this book could you kindly leave us a positive review?

COLOR TEST PAGE

A BIG
Thank you!

If you enjoyed this book could you kindly leave us a positive review?

Made in the USA
Monee, IL
02 December 2024

72007060R00063